THE USBORNE
FIRST BOOK OF THE
RECORDER

Philip Hawthorn

Edited by Janet Cook and Judy Tatchell
Designed and illustrated by Kim Blundell

Consultant: Stephanie Roberts
Original music by Philip Hawthorn

Contents

About this book

There are lots of different types of recorder. This book is all about the soprano recorder. You can find out how to read music so that you can play tunes on your recorder.

You can discover how music is written down and there are explanations of music words and symbols. Throughout the book there are pieces of music for you to practice, and puzzles to do.

The book shows you how to play different musical sounds, or notes, on your recorder. Each page with a new note has a red corner with the note's name on it. You can look them up quickly and easily.

There are 18 whole pages of tunes, from pop songs to Christmas carols. Some are written so that you can play them with a friend. You will know many of the tunes already. Others have been written especially for this book.

The book also contains some amazing stories and facts about the recorder. For instance, what does King Henry VIII of England have to do with recorder music? What are the biggest and smallest recorders in the world?

At the end of the book you can read about other members of the recorder family. There is also a table showing you the different brands of soprano recorder. This will help you if you are thinking of buying one.

About your recorder

There are four main sizes of recorder. These are the sopranino (the smallest), soprano, alto and tenor (the biggest).* This book is about the soprano recorder. It is about one foot (30cm) long.

Soprano recorders are made of plastic or wood. Most have two or three sections, called joints, which fit together.

The different parts of a recorder

Here is a picture of a recorder which has three joints. The picture tells you what each part is for and what it is called.

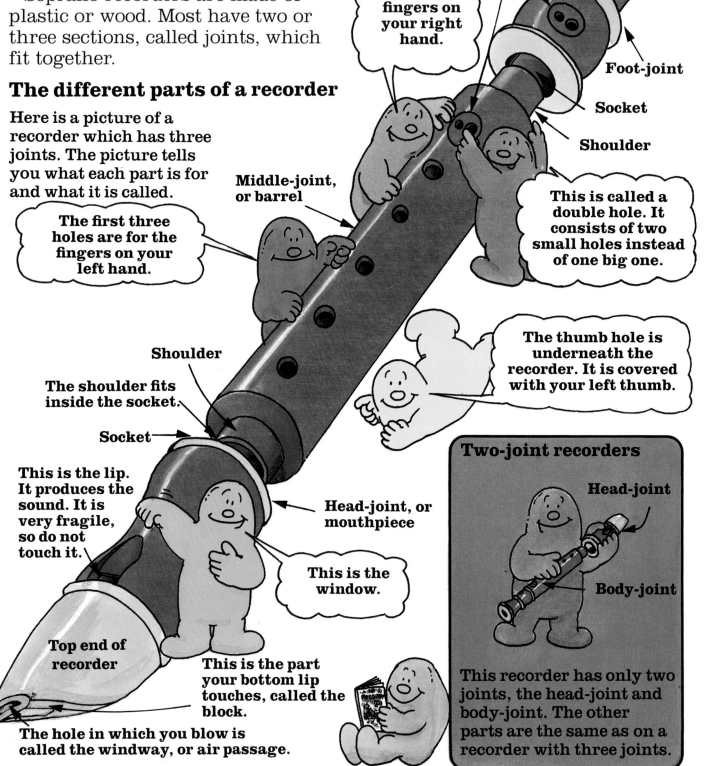

Each double hole is covered by one finger.

Bottom end of recorder

The bottom four holes are for the fingers on your right hand.

Foot-joint

Socket

Shoulder

This is called a double hole. It consists of two small holes instead of one big one.

Middle-joint, or barrel

The first three holes are for the fingers on your left hand.

The thumb hole is underneath the recorder. It is covered with your left thumb.

Shoulder

The shoulder fits inside the socket.

Socket

This is the lip. It produces the sound. It is very fragile, so do not touch it.

Head-joint, or mouthpiece

This is the window.

Top end of recorder

This is the part your bottom lip touches, called the block.

The hole in which you blow is called the windway, or air passage.

Two-joint recorders

Head-joint

Body-joint

This recorder has only two joints, the head-joint and body-joint. The other parts are the same as on a recorder with three joints.

4   *You can find out about these on page 60.

Taking your recorder apart...   ...and putting it together

> If the joints get stiff, you can buy some grease from a music shop to rub on to them.

Hold the head-joint firmly in one hand. Hold the middle-joint (or body-joint if your recorder has two parts) in the other.

Gently twist the joints and pull them apart. If your recorder has three parts, do the same with the foot-joint.

Hold the head-joint and middle-joint (or body-joint) firmly. Carefully insert the shoulder into the socket and twist the joints.

Line up the holes with the window. If you have a three-joint recorder, set the holes on the foot-joint slightly to the right.

Looking after your recorder

It is important that you look after your recorder carefully. It can very easily get damaged. If it does, it may not produce such a good sound. Here are a few tips for taking care of your recorder.

Mop

Slit

Cleaning rod

> Never grip the recorder between your teeth. It may make the hole in the mouthpiece smaller and harder to blow.

1. Always clean the inside of your recorder after you have finished playing it. The cleaning tools for this are the mop and cleaning rod.

> One of these is sometimes included with your recorder when you buy it.

2. You need to insert a piece of cloth in the slit at the end of a cleaning rod. Part of an old handkerchief will do.

> Do not store your recorder in direct sunlight or anywhere too warm. It may go out of shape.

> Always keep your recorder in a bag when you are not playing it. This will prevent it from getting scratched or blocked with dust.

5

Holding and blowing your recorder

On these two pages you can find out how to hold and blow your recorder. Doing these things properly will help you to play it better.

Holding your recorder

Below are some tips which will help you hold your recorder comfortably and properly. You can sit or stand when playing.

Hold your recorder half way between straight out and straight down.

Prop up this book in front of you. If you have to bend over to read the book, it may be difficult to breathe properly when you start playing.

Leave a slight gap between your elbows and your body.

Always sit or stand straight. Relax and take care not to hunch your shoulders.

Making a sound

Now you are ready to blow your recorder. First, try it without covering any holes. To do this, hold your recorder by the mouthpiece, as in the picture.

Take a deep breath. Now blow gently and you will hear a sound.

Take care not to blow too hard or you will make the recorder squeak.

If the air passage gets blocked with moisture from your breath, put your finger across the window and blow sharply.

Try to keep the stream of air steady.

If you do not blow hard enough, or run out of breath, the note will sound like a vacuum cleaner being turned off.

Using your tongue when you blow

Before you blow, place your tongue just behind your top teeth. Say "too" as you blow gently into the recorder.

Hold the note for a few seconds. Then put your tongue back behind your teeth as you stop blowing.

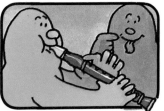

Using your tongue like this is called tonguing. It gives the notes you play a crisp beginning and end.

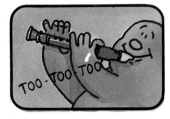

Try to play a series of notes by saying "too-too-too-too" into the recorder. Hold each note for about a second.

Where your fingers go

Keep your right thumb here all the time.

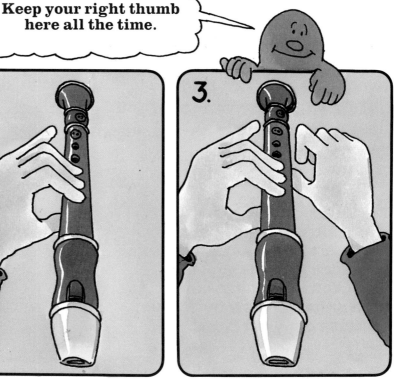

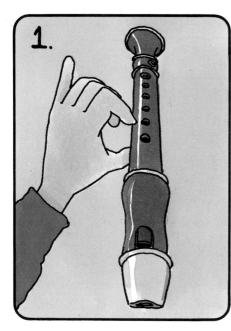

1.

Start with the fingering for your left hand. First place your left thumb over the thumb hole under the recorder.

2.

Now place your first three fingers over the first three holes as shown above. You do not use the little finger on your left hand.

3.

Next put your right thumb underneath the recorder, between holes four and five. This helps to support the recorder.

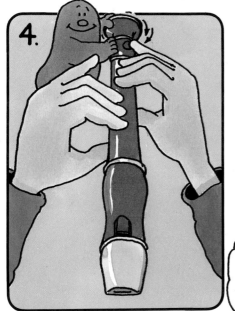

4.

Your four right-hand fingers cover the remaining holes. If your recorder has three joints, twist the foot-joint so that your little finger can reach it more easily.

5.

You do not need to press very hard when you are playing tunes.

Make sure your fingers cover the holes completely. Otherwise, air will escape when you blow. Check this by putting your fingers and thumb on their holes and pressing hard.

6.

The mark on your thumb should be slightly to one side.

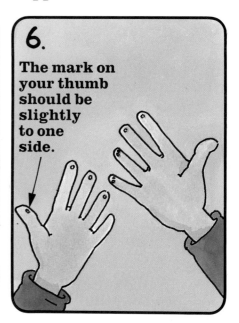

Now take them off. Each hole will make a mark on your finger. The marks should be in the center of each finger. Practice until you can get the marks in the right place.

All about musical notes

Music is made up of lots of notes. On these two pages you can find out how to play your first note on the recorder.

What are notes like?

Some notes are high and others are low. A note lasts for as long as you blow. You can change how high or low a note is by covering different holes.

Playing your first note

1. Put your left thumb on the thumb hole underneath the recorder. Place your first finger on the hole nearest to the mouthpiece.

2. Make sure that you have covered the two holes completely. Also, take care not to cover any other holes by mistake.

3. Support your recorder with your right-hand thumb. Do not hold the foot-joint. The other fingers should be about one inch (2.5cm) above their holes.

4. Blow into the recorder using your tongue as shown on page 6. You have now played your first note.

5. All notes are named after the first seven letters of the alphabet. The note you have played is B.

Cover with your first finger. **B**

Cover with your left thumb.

Every time you learn a new note, there will be a picture like the one above. It tells you the note's name and which holes to cover.

Playing a rhythm

All music has a rhythm. A rhythm is made up of a series of beats. The ticking of a clock and the beating of your heart are both rhythms.

Each note you are playing is a B with a length of one beat.

Say the words in the box above. Try and make each word last the same length of time.

Now try clapping your hands as you say each word. Each of your claps is one beat.

You are clapping the simplest rhythm, where all the beats are the same length.

Say the words in your head and play a B on your recorder for each word.

Music symbols

There is a music symbol for notes of one beat. It is called a quarter note. You can see a picture of one on the right.

This is a quarter note. There are other music symbols to show when a note is longer or shorter than one beat. You can find out about them on the next few pages.

Quarter note

This word has two syllables.

These quarter notes are one beat long.

Make sure you tongue each note.

Above are some more words. You can see that the longer words are split into two parts. Each part is called a syllable.

Say the words, keeping a steady rhythm. Each short word has one quarter note beat. So does each syllable of the longer words.

Say the words again, clapping as you say each one. The quarter notes show that each word or syllable is one beat long.

Play this one-note tune using B. The quarter notes show that each note is the same length. Practice this a few times.

B

Writing notes down

Music is written down so that people can read and play it. Note symbols are written on a set of lines, called a staff.

The letters for the spaces spell FACE.

A way to remember the note names of the staff lines is to learn a special phrase like the one below.

Each word begins with the letter-name of a line, starting with the bottom one.

The staff

Treble clef

The name of this note is B. It is one beat long.

Space   Line

A staff is a bit like a ladder. The higher up the staff you go, the higher the notes are.

Enormous Green Boots Don't Fit

Above is a staff. It is made up of five lines. Each different note has its own place on the staff. Some go on the lines and others in the spaces.

The letters in the picture above are the names of the notes. Notice that there are two Es and two Fs.* To write B you put a note symbol on the middle line.

The symbol at the beginning of the staff is a treble clef. You will see it at the beginning of all staffs of soprano recorder music.

Another rhythm to clap

This word lasts for two beats. It is like saying "le-eft".

Left,	right,	left
(clap)	(clap)	(clap)

Sol	- diers	mar	- ching
(clap)	(clap)	(clap)	(clap)

Left,	right,	left	
(clap)	(clap)	(clap)	(silent clap)

Sol	- diers	mar	- ching
(clap)	(clap)	(clap)	(clap)

Say these words, making each the same length. Now clap your hands as you say each word. There are three claps on the first line and four on the second.

The rhythm might sound better if the lines had the same number of beats. You can make the top line four beats long by giving the word at the end two beats.

Say and clap the words again. Keep your claps the same length. On the word "three", clap once and count an extra beat in your head.

You can find out why on page 24.

Two-beat notes

A half note is worth two quarter notes. One half note lasts for two beats.

The symbol which shows a note is two beats long is called a half note. It looks like a white quarter note.

Here is a tune for the words on the previous page written on a staff. Play it on your recorder.

Count the numbers in your head as you play to help keep the rhythm regular.

Dividing up the music

This 4 tells you how many beats are in each bar.

This 4 stands for quarter notes. So there are 4 quarter notes to a bar.

This bar has 1+1+2=4 beats.

Bar line

This bar has 1+1+1+1=4 beats.

One bar

Music is divided up into sections, called bars. Each bar contains the same number of beats.

The numbers after the treble clef will tell you how many beats are in each bar. They are called the time signature.

The last bar line is always a double one. This tells you that the tune is finished.

A tune with half notes

Here is another tune. Clap the rhythm then play the tune on your recorder.

How many bars are there in this tune?

If this bar were full of quarter notes how many would there be?

Count two beats for each of these half notes.

The beats in the bar are numbered.

Answers on page 63.

Some more notes

On these two pages you can find out about the note A. You can also learn about a four-beat note length called a whole note.

Playing the note A

Put your fingers on the recorder as if you were going to play a B. Now put your left-hand middle finger on the second hole. This is A.

Practice lifting and replacing your middle finger. Keep your other fingers about an inch (2.5cm) above their holes.

A

The black dots show which holes to cover.

The note A is written in the space just below the B line. As it sounds lower than B, it is lower down on the staff.

Say the words in your head as you play the notes.

Old B New A

Say the words, clap the rhythm and play the notes written above. Listen how A is lower than B. Play the bar a number of times.

Four-beat notes

A whole note is worth four quarter notes. There are two half notes in a whole note.

Whole note

Just as there are symbols for one-beat and two-beat notes, there is also one for a four-beat note. It is like a half note without a tail, and is called a whole note.

Say it

Clap it

Play it

Who — le note in this song,

It's — ve — ry Long —

Try playing the tune above. Don't forget to count four beats for the whole note.

Notice that the time signature is just at the beginning of the tune.

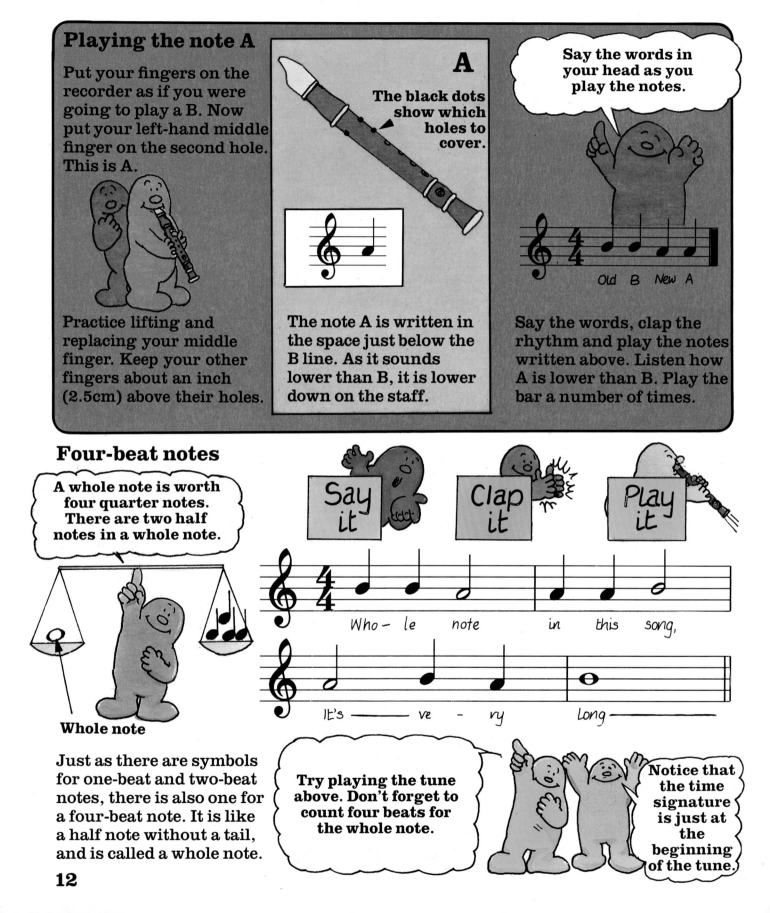

12

Leaving gaps in music

In some music there are gaps when no sound is made. These are called rests. Rests can last for any number of beats. There is a symbol for each length of rest. Below are the rest symbols for the note lengths you have learned so far.

Note symbol	Length in beats	Rest symbol
Whole note	4	
Half note	2	
Quarter note	1	

When you see a rest, count the right beats in your head without playing a note.

The whole note rest is strong, so it can hang from the line.

The half note rest is weak; it needs to sit on the line.

This is a quarter note rest. Remember to leave a gap of one beat.

Rest game

Ice cold cream cakes

Here is a game to help you practice using rests. Say the words and clap the rhythm.

Ice cold cream (*rest*)

Here, the last beat has been replaced by a quarter note rest. When you get to the rest, do not clap. Instead, say "rest" silently in your head.

Ice (*rest*) cream (*rest*)

Now try replacing the second quarter note with a rest.

A tune with rests

The music below has rests in it. Say the words, clap the rhythm, then play the tune.

Hopscotch

Don't rush this half note rest. Count in time with the rest of the music.

Play-ing play-ing   hop-scotch   Oh   hur-ry up and   throw,

Hop and step you   touched the line   you are out   my   go!

A

Taking breaths

When you play your recorder, it is important to breathe in the right places so you do not interrupt the flow of the music. There are symbols, called breath marks, which tell you when to take a breath.

1. When you take a breath, keep the recorder resting on your bottom lip.

2. Breathe in quickly through your mouth. Try not to make a noise.

3. Make sure you do not blow too hard after you have taken a breath.

> If you do not breathe regularly, the music will sound wobbly. You might even feel dizzy.

This is a breath mark. It looks like a "check".

Clap the rhythm and then play the tune above. Breathe when you get to the breath mark over the second bar line.

It is always best to take a breath at a mark even if you do not need to. This is because it may be a while until the next breath mark.

Playing G

G

GABG

> These are the note names to help you remember them.

Put your fingers on your recorder as if you were going to play A. Now put the third finger of your left hand on the next hole. This is the fingering for G.

G is written on the second line up on the staff.

Play the bar above a number of times. It will help you practice moving your fingers. Notice that as notes on the staff go up and down, so do the sounds.

Dotted notes

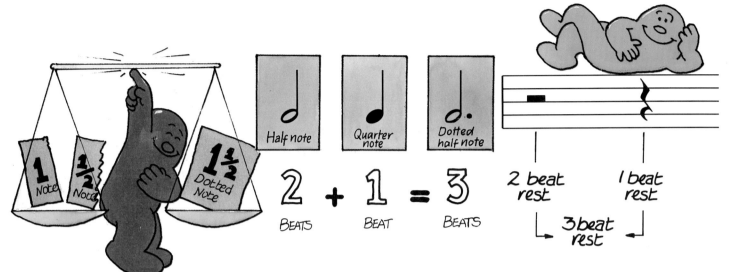

A dot after a note means it lasts half as long again. Here you can find out what a dotted half note sounds like.

A dotted half note is three beats long. There are two beats for the half note, with an extra one beat (length of a quarter note) added.

A rest lasting for three beats is shown by a half note rest followed by a quarter note rest.

Tune with dotted half notes

Below is a tune which includes dotted half notes. It has a 3/4 time signature. This means that there are three quarter note beats in each bar. Clap the rhythm before you play the tune to help you get it right.

Remember to count three beats for these dotted half notes.

Cuckoo Song

If you count these numbers in your head, they will help you keep time.

Short notes

Up until now the tunes in this book have been made up of notes which last for one, two, three or four beats. There is also a shorter note, called an eighth note. Eighth notes are half a beat in length.

Eighth notes

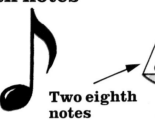

Two eighth notes

1 Above you can see a picture of an eighth note. It is like a quarter note with a tail.

2 Two eighth notes are the same length as one quarter note.

3 When two or more eighth notes are next to each other, their tails can be joined.

4 The picture above shows an eighth note rest. It tells you to leave a gap of half a beat before playing the next note.

Rhythms with eighth notes

Say the words written below, then clap the rhythms.

Rhythms do not need to be written on a staff. Can you think why?*

4/4 Once in a blue moon.

3/4 La - ven - ders blue dil-ly dil-ly La - ven - ders green.

4/4 Fred-die had a fright in the mid-dle of the night.

16 *Answer on page 63.*

Answer on page 63.

Playing and reading E

Put your fingers on your recorder as if you were going to play a G. Now place the first two fingers of your right hand on the next two holes.

Remember to use your tongue to start and finish the note.

Blow very gently so you do not make a squeak. Lower notes do not need as much breath as higher ones.

E

The note E is written on the bottom line of the staff.

Play this bar a few times.

Practice playing G and E. Make sure you lift and replace both right-hand fingers together.

A tune with eighth notes

Here is a tune for you to play. Clap the rhythm before you play it. The numbers underneath the notes will help you count the beats. When you clap two eighth notes, say an "and" for the second one.

Here are four eighth notes joined together.

Indian Dance

This is short for "and".

Starting with part of a bar

Some tunes start with part of a bar instead of a whole one. This part is called an anacrusis. There is an anacrusis in the tune below.

Count in your head the "missing" beats before the anacrusis so that you don't lose the rhythm in the bars following it.

When there is an anacrusis, the last bar is made up of the "missing" beats from the beginning.

Go! Stop!

Count three beats so you can tell when to start the tune.

This is an anacrusis. It is one beat long.

The last bar has only three beats as there is a one beat anacrusis at the beginning.

If the anacrusis at the beginning of the tune were two beats long, how many beats would be in the last bar?*

This must have been the first *rock* music!

Amazing recorder fact

The earliest recorder which has ever been found was made between 25,000 and 22,000BC. This was the time when people lived in caves.

This recorder was made out of a piece of animal bone.

E

Tying notes together

Sometimes two or more notes on the same line or space are joined together with a curved line. These are called tied notes.

With tied notes you only play one note even though you can see two. The note lasts as long as the two added together.

Tied notes

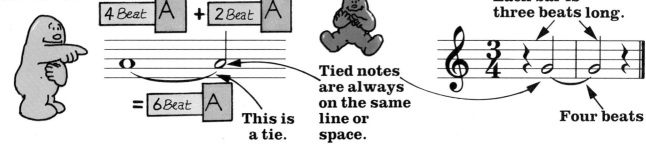

4 Beat A + **2 Beat A**

= **6 Beat A**

This is a tie.

Tied notes are always on the same line or space.

Each bar is three beats long.

Four beats

Above are a whole note and half note which are tied. Instead of playing an A with four beats and then another with two, you play one A with six beats.

Tied notes can stretch across any number of bar lines. In the music above, the note is four beats long even though the bar length is three beats.

Count the beats

On the right are some tied notes. Their total lengths are written underneath them. Can you work out the missing totals correctly?*

3 BEATS   **4 BEATS**   **?**   **?**

Playing and reading D

Place your fingers on the recorder as if you were going to play an E (see page 16). Now put the third finger of your right hand over the first double hole. Make sure you cover both small holes.

You can see why there are two small holes on page 44.

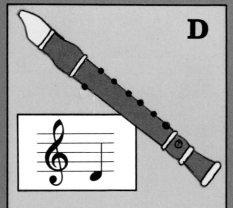

D

The note D is written in the space just underneath the staff.

D G E G

A D G

Note names

Practice the bars written above. Remember to use your tongue.

18   *Answers on page 63.*

Dotted quarter notes

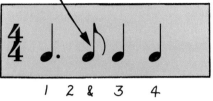

Dotted quarter note

A dot after a note makes it half as long again. A dotted quarter note is one and a half beats.

A dotted quarter note can be written as a tied quarter note and eighth note. But it is often written with a dot.

Clap this eighth note on the "and" between beats two and three.

Try clapping the rhythm above. Count the numbers in your head to help you keep time.

Tunes to play

Below are two tunes for you to play. Remember to look out for the tied notes.

Clap it...

...then play it.

Remember to breathe at the breath marks.

Play this tune quite quickly.

English Folk Song

Hawthorn

These tied notes have three beats.

Merrily we roll along

American

D

Repeating music

In some tunes there are two symbols which tell you to play some or all of the music again. These symbols are called repeat marks. There is a picture of them on the right.

Repeat marks

Repeating music in the middle of a tune

When you see two repeat marks in a tune, you play everything between them again. Follow the steps in the tune below to see how this works.

1. You ignore this sign the first time you see it.

These two bars are in between the two repeat marks.

2. Go back to the first repeat sign.

3. Play the music from here again.

Start here.

If the bars in the tune above were numbered, this is the order in which you would play them.

1 2 3 4
3 4 5 6

4. You ignore this sign the second time you get to it and play the rest of the tune.

Repeating a tune from the beginning

Sometimes a tune only contains the second type of repeat mark. (This has dots on the left.) It tells you to go back to the beginning and play everything again. You can see this below.

On the right of the music you can see in which order you would play the bars of the tune.

Play all the bars before the repeat sign again.

Go back to the beginning.

Repeat marks are usually written in place of a bar line.

You ignore the sign the second time and play to the end of the tune.

BAR ORDER
1 2 1 2
3 4 5 6

Repeat marks game

Here are three sets of bar lines and repeat marks. Each bar has a number instead of notes.

Can you work out the order of the bars?*

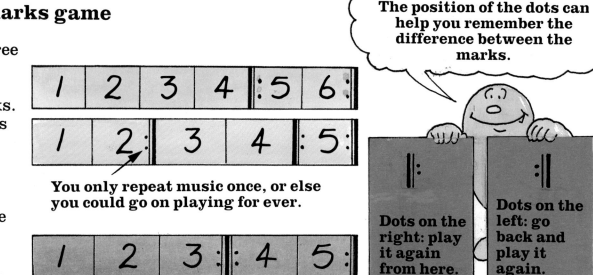

You only repeat music once, or else you could go on playing for ever.

The position of the dots can help you remember the difference between the marks.

Dots on the right: play it again from here.

Dots on the left: go back and play it again.

Playing and reading C

Put your fingers on the recorder as if you were going to play an A (see page 12). Now lift your first finger, leaving your thumb and middle finger on the recorder. This is the fingering for a C.

Keep your other fingers ready to cover their holes.

You only need your left-hand fingers to play C, but support your recorder with your right thumb.

C is written in the third space up from the bottom of the staff. Notes above the middle line have their tails pointing down.

Practice these bars.

The note B can have its tail pointing upwards or downwards.

This C is often written C′. You can see why on page 24.

First and second endings

Sometimes, a repeated section has two different endings. Below, you play the bar marked "1." the first time. The second time you skip over it and play "2."

Play this bar the first time through.

Play this bar the second time through.

When you can play this tune, try the two tunes on the opposite page.

*The answers are on page 63.

C′

In-between notes

Although two notes may have letter-names which are next to each other in the alphabet, there may be another note in between them. In-between notes are called sharp or flat notes. On the next three pages you can find out about sharp notes*.

Sharp notes

A sharp note is half-way between two letter-name notes. It is slightly higher than one note and slightly lower than the other.

F sharp is slightly higher than F.

A sharp note is slightly higher than the note it takes its name from. In the picture above you can see F sharp.

Sharp sign.

There is a sign for a sharp note. You can see one above. The sign is placed after the letter, so F sharp is written F#.

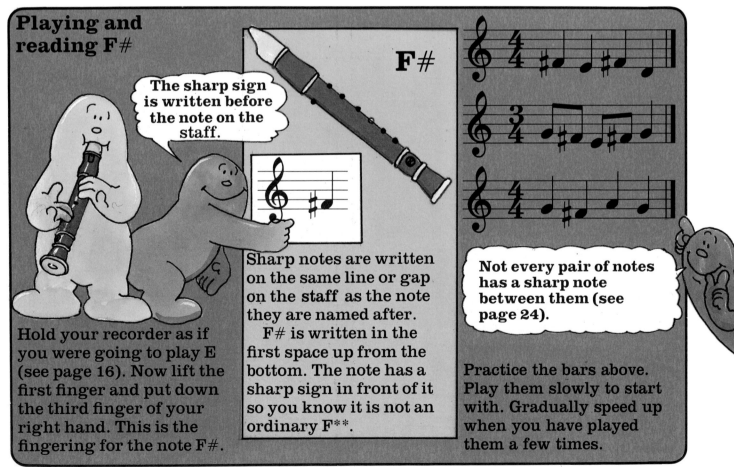

Playing and reading F#

The sharp sign is written before the note on the staff.

F#

Hold your recorder as if you were going to play E (see page 16). Now lift the first finger and put down the third finger of your right hand. This is the fingering for the note F#.

Sharp notes are written on the same line or gap on the staff as the note they are named after.

F# is written in the first space up from the bottom. The note has a sharp sign in front of it so you know it is not an ordinary F**.

Not every pair of notes has a sharp note between them (see page 24).

Practice the bars above. Play them slowly to start with. Gradually speed up when you have played them a few times.

*See page 36 for more about flat notes.
**You can find out how to play F on page 34.

A new time signature

Some tunes have a time signature called 6/8. The six tells you that you count six to a bar. The eight tells you that you count in eighth notes. This is similar to 3/4 time, which has three quarter notes (the same number of beats as six eighth notes). The difference is in the way the eighth notes are grouped.

IN   the   MONTH   of   AP - ril

pulse 1   pulse 2   pulse 3

Each pulse comes on the first of a pair of two eighth notes.

SI - lent - ly   SI - lent - ly

pulse 1   pulse 2

These pulses come on the first of a group of three eighth notes.

★ In 3/4 time, the eighth notes are in three sets of two. This gives the rhythm three strong pulses. Say the words below the eighth notes. The syllables in capitals are the three pulses.

★ In 6/8 time the eighth notes are grouped into two sets of three. Say the words under these eighth notes. They have a slightly different rhythm. There are only two pulses.

Tunes in 6/8 time

Below are two tunes which have a 6/8 time signature. Clap them, then play them. The numbers under the staff will help you to get the right rhythm.

There is another sharp sign here. Each sharp only affects the bar it is in.

Fairground Ride

This sharp sign makes all F notes in the bar into F#. So you only need one sharp sign for both F notes.

In 6/8 time, you count six to a bar.

Drink to me only with thine eyes   English

Although this F sharp sign is on the top line, all F notes are played as F sharp.

This tune has a sharp sign written on the F line at the beginning of the staff.   This means that all F notes in the F space at the bottom are converted to   F#. It affects every bar in the tune.

F#

The note ladder

In the picture below is a ladder which shows all the notes you can learn to play in this book. The higher they are on the ladder, the higher they sound.

Notes with the same letter names

You can see that some notes have the same letter name as others. To help you tell which is which, the lower one is called "low" and the higher one, "high".

For instance the C note at the bottom of the ladder is often called low C, and the other one just over half way up is called high C.

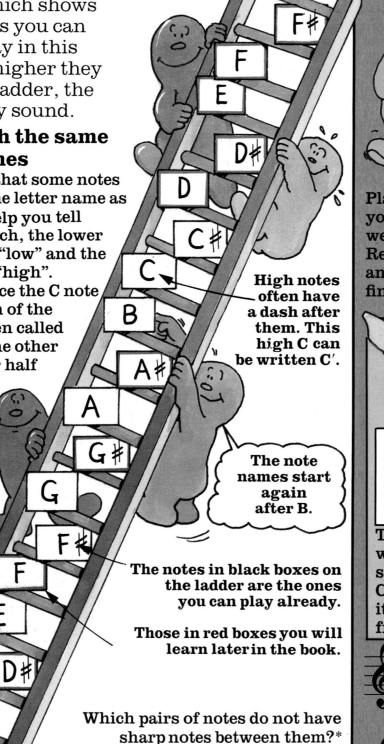

How many different notes are there?*

High notes often have a dash after them. This high C can be written C′.

The note names start again after B.

The notes in black boxes on the ladder are the ones you can play already.

Those in red boxes you will learn later in the book.

Which pairs of notes do not have sharp notes between them?*

The lowest note that you can play on your recorder is low C. You can find out how to play it on page 33.

*Answer on page 63.

24

Playing and reading high C#

Blow carefully as it can easily sound out of tune.

Place your fingers on your recorder as if you were going to play an A. Remove your left thumb, and you have the fingering for C#′.

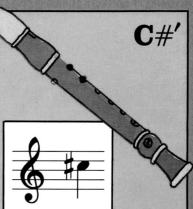

C#′

The note C#′ is written in the same space as high C (or C′). As it is a sharp, it has a sharp sign in front of it.

Play the bars above to help you get used to the new note.

Playing and reading high D

Don't mix up high D with low D (see page 18).

D′

Place your fingers on the recorder as if you were going to play a C#. Now remove your first finger. This is the fingering for high D.

High D, or D′, is written on the fourth line up from the bottom of the staff. The tail of the note hangs down.

Play the bars above. Listen to how low D and high D sound similar. Can you hear how C# is in between C and D?

A tune to practice

Below is a tune for you to play.

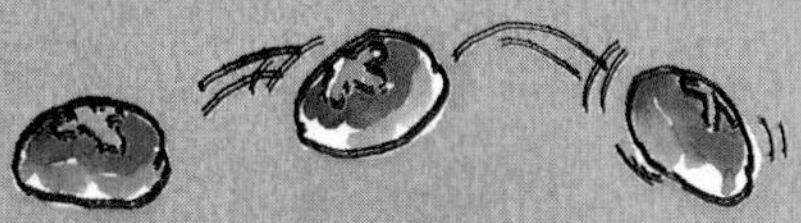

Hot Cross Buns   English

Royal recorders

In the late fifteenth century, recorders were one of the most popular instruments in Europe.

The English King Henry VII had several recorder players in his court. When he told them to play, they could choose from up to 16 recorders of different sizes which they kept in a large chest.

D′
C#′

Tunes to play

On these two pages are some tunes to play. You may have heard some of them before. They will help you to practice what you have learned in the book so far.

Make sure you get the rhythms right by clapping the tunes before you play them on your recorder.

Au clair de la lune   **French**

G G G A

C   C   C

German Song   **Hawthorn**

A tune for one or two players

This sort of tune is called a round. It is written so that two people can play it at the same time, but at different places in the music. You can either play this tune by yourself, or with someone else who plays the recorder. If you are playing the tune with someone else, it will help if you both practice by yourselves first.

Folk Round

Second player starts at the beginning when you get to here.

You begin the tune. When you get to the red arrow, your friend starts playing from the beginning while you continue the tune.

When you get to the end, you can repeat the tune as many times as you like. Make sure you listen to each other to help you keep in time.

When the saints go marchin' in American

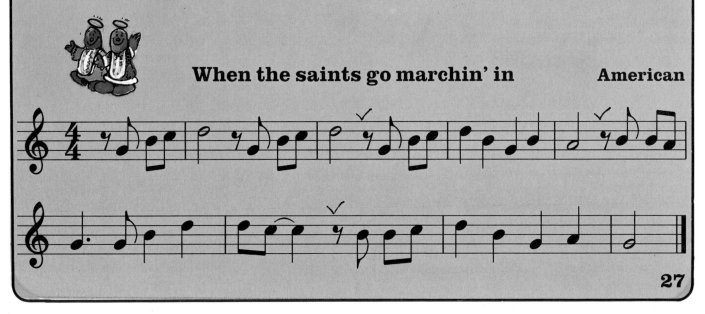

Playing a scale

A scale is made up of eight different notes played one after the other. It begins and ends on notes with the same letter name.

The word scale comes from the Italian word *scala* which means ladder. You can imagine that playing a scale is like climbing up or down part of the note ladder shown on page 24, treading on certain rungs. You can find out more about scales below.

The scale of D

On this ladder, you can see which notes make up the scale of D*. It starts on low D and ends on high D. It is sometimes called the scale of D major.

> **Only the notes in red boxes are in the scale of D.**

Below, the scale of D is written on a staff. Play it slowly. Notice how the notes get higher, like climbing the ladder.

This is where A# would be.

> **A semitone is like taking a small step of one rung. A tone is like taking a big step of two rungs.**

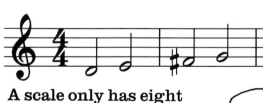

A scale only has eight notes, so not all the notes between low D and high D are in the scale of D. The notes in red are in the scale.

> **If there are notes which you have forgotten how to play, look them up.**

28   *On page 42, you can learn how to work out which notes are in other scales.

Writing the sharps at the beginning

The scale of D can be written with the sharp signs next to the treble clef. You can see this on the right.

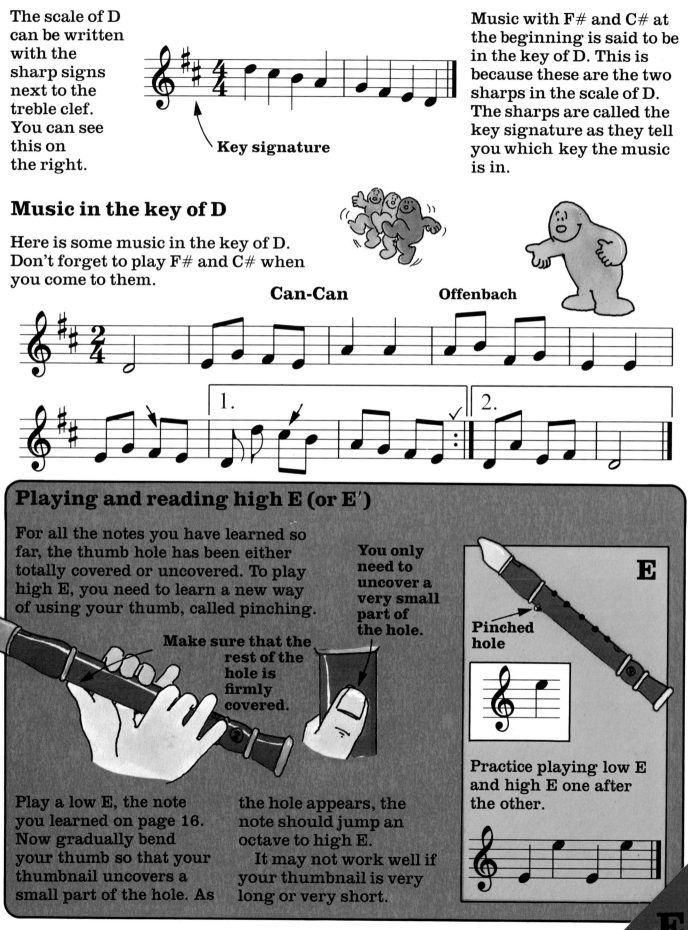

Key signature

Music with F# and C# at the beginning is said to be in the key of D. This is because these are the two sharps in the scale of D. The sharps are called the key signature as they tell you which key the music is in.

Music in the key of D

Here is some music in the key of D. Don't forget to play F# and C# when you come to them.

Can-Can   **Offenbach**

Playing and reading high E (or E′)

For all the notes you have learned so far, the thumb hole has been either totally covered or uncovered. To play high E, you need to learn a new way of using your thumb, called pinching.

You only need to uncover a very small part of the hole.

Make sure that the rest of the hole is firmly covered.

Pinched hole

E

Play a low E, the note you learned on page 16. Now gradually bend your thumb so that your thumbnail uncovers a small part of the hole. As the hole appears, the note should jump an octave to high E.

It may not work well if your thumbnail is very long or very short.

Practice playing low E and high E one after the other.

E′

Musical instructions

You can make music sound more interesting by playing notes in different ways. For example, loudly or quietly, smoothly or jerkily. The next few pages show you how, and explain the words and symbols which tell you how to play.

Music words and symbols

This is some 15th century music.

The music words and symbols which describe how to play a tune are in Italian. This is because the way music is written today was mostly invented by an Italian called Guido d'Arezzo (995-1050). His way of writing music was later developed in Italy in the 15th century.

Playing smooth notes

The Italian word for smoothly is *legato*. It is pronounced "le-ga-toe".

Tongue this note.

Tongue the next note, but don't stop blowing.

There are more Italian words on page 40.

Lullabies are often played *legato*.

legato

To play music *legato,* use your tongue to start each note. Hold it as long as possible, then gently tongue the next note. Don't stop blowing between notes.

Above is a bar of music which should be played *legato*. To tell you this, the word "legato" is written underneath the staff.

Playing separate notes

Try not to speed up the notes. Keep them on the beats.

Don't mix up *staccato* notes with dotted notes (see page 15).

Staccato note   Dotted note

Some music tells you to play notes separately, which makes music sound jerky. The word for this is *staccato*, pronounced "sta-ca-toe". Staccato notes are written with a dot underneath (or on top if their tails point down).

Above are some *staccato* notes. Say "tut" instead of "too". This makes your tongue stop the note as well as start it.

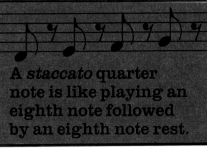

A *staccato* quarter note is like playing an eighth note followed by an eighth note rest.

Slurred notes

Slurred notes are at different places on the staff.

Tied notes are on the same line or space.

Notes on different lines or spaces with a curved line underneath them are called slurred notes. They run on from one to the other with no tonguing in between. The line is a slur.

Slurred notes are different from tied notes (see page 18) because they are not on the same line or space on the staff.

Slurred notes **Tied notes**

Tongue the first note.

Change the fingering without tonguing.

Try to move your fingers neatly or you may play some other notes by mistake.

When you play slurred notes, you only tongue the first one. The rest are played by just moving your fingers while you continue to blow.

The staff above shows two slurred notes. Tongue the first one (low G). After two beats, lift the third finger of your right hand to play low F. Don't use your tongue to start the second note.

What is the difference between *legato* notes and slurred notes?*

legato

Don't stop blowing between these slurred notes.

A tune using slurs

Below is a tune which has some slurs. Don't forget to tongue the first note only.

Tongue this note.

Cat and Mouse

Hawthorn

These are *staccato* notes.

Answer on page 63.

Playing loudly and quietly

Some tunes are suited to being played loudly and others quietly. For example, a march should be played loudly.

There are three levels of loudness and three of quietness. Each level has its own Italian term.

Quiet music

The three levels of quietness are very quiet, quiet and moderately (or fairly) quiet. The Italian word for quiet is *piano*, pronounced "pee-ya-no". The terms for all three levels are based on the word *piano*.

Loud music

The three terms for loudness are similar to the ones for quietness: moderately loud, loud and very loud. The Italian word for loud is *forte*, pronounced "for-tay". Below are the terms for the three levels.

pianissimo | piano | mezzo piano | mezzo forte | forte | fortissimo

Writing "issimo" after a word means "very". So pianissimo means "very quiet".

Mezzo (pronounced "met-zo") means moderately. So mezzo piano means moderately quiet.

A way to remember what mezzo means, is that it starts with the same letter as "moderately".

Loud and quiet instructions

pianissimo	piano	mezzo piano	mezzo forte	forte	fortissimo
pp	**p**	**mp**	**mf**	**f**	**ff**

The instructions as to how loudly or quietly you play are written as one or two letters under the staff.

This table tells you what they are. There is usually an instruction at the beginning of a tune. There

may be others during it as well. In the tune above, you begin very quietly then change to loud.

How to play loudly and quietly

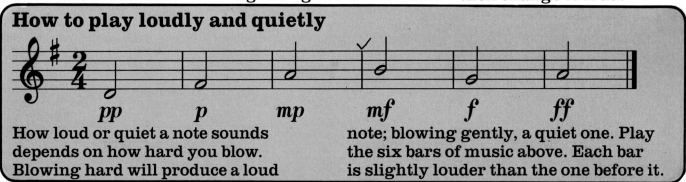

pp   p   mp   mf   f   ff

How loud or quiet a note sounds depends on how hard you blow. Blowing hard will produce a loud

note; blowing gently, a quiet one. Play the six bars of music above. Each bar is slightly louder than the one before it.

32

Very short notes

An eighth note equals two sixteenth notes.

1 beat   1 beat   1 beat

Sixteenth notes can be joined together with two lines.

1 In the picture above, the right pan contains some sixteenth notes. They each have two tails. A sixteenth note is half an eighth note and is a quarter of a beat long.

2 Clap the rhythm above. Each group of notes is one beat long. When you're clapping, try to keep each note the same length.

too   too   too-goo-too-goo

3 Sixteenth note tails can be joined to eighth note tails. Try clapping the rhythms above.

4 Sixteenth notes can be hard to tongue crisply. You may find it helpful to say "too-goo-too-goo" as you play them.

A tune with sixteenth notes

The Keeper   **English**

too-goo   too-goo

too-goo-too-goo   too-goo

Here is a tune with some sixteenth notes. Clap it first, then play it. The words underneath will help you tongue the notes accurately.

Playing and reading low C

Low C is the lowest note you can play on a soprano recorder. Finger low D, then place your right-hand little finger on its hole.

On some recorders you can twist the foot-joint so it is easier to reach the bottom holes.

Make sure you cover both small holes.

Blow gently as it is easy to squeak with this note. Practise moving your little finger up and down.

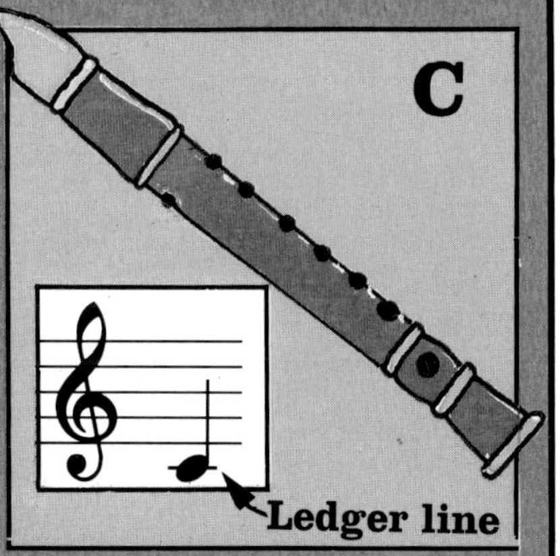

C

Ledger line

Low C is written below the staff on a special line called a ledger line. Ledger lines are used for very high or low notes.

Practice the bar below.

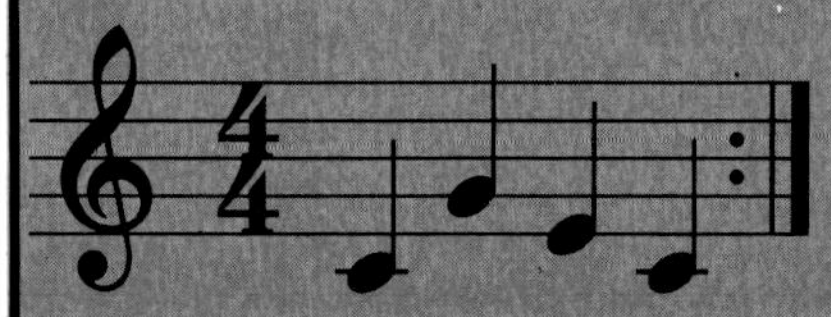

C

Natural notes

Natural sign

A natural note is any note which is not a sharp or a flat. A natural sign cancels out the effect of these signs. Below you can find out the two occasions when this happens.

1 A natural sign in a bar cancels the effect of a sharp or flat sign earlier in the bar.

This would be C# if it did not have a natural sign next to it.

C sharp

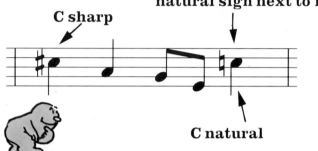

C natural

In the bar above, the first note is C sharp. The fourth is C natural because it has a natural sign next to it.

2 A sharp sign on a line or space at the beginning of the staff makes every note with the same name into a sharp. A natural sign turns them back into naturals.

Key signature   F natural

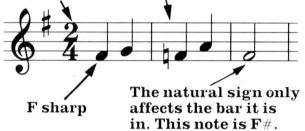

F sharp

The natural sign only affects the bar it is in. This note is F#.

The F in the first bar above is F sharp. In the second bar, the natural sign makes the note F natural.

Playing and reading low F

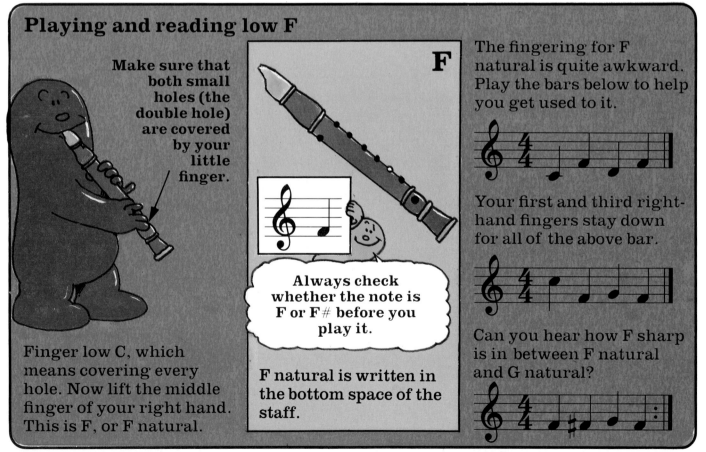

Make sure that both small holes (the double hole) are covered by your little finger.

Finger low C, which means covering every hole. Now lift the middle finger of your right hand. This is F, or F natural.

Always check whether the note is F or F# before you play it.

F natural is written in the bottom space of the staff.

The fingering for F natural is quite awkward. Play the bars below to help you get used to it.

Your first and third right-hand fingers stay down for all of the above bar.

Can you hear how F sharp is in between F natural and G natural?

Scale of C major

You now know how to play all the notes in the scale of C major. This ladder shows the notes in the scale.

The notes run from low C to high C.

Here are the notes on the staff. Practice playing them up and down. There are no sharps in the scale.

Now you know two scales: C major and D major. Practice them each time you play your recorder.

The key of C major

On page 28 you learnt that the scale of D major had two sharps in it.

C major has no sharps or flats. This means that any tunes which have no sharp or flat signs at the beginning are in the key of C major.

Key of D major

Key of C major

Tunes to play

Here are two tunes. Watch out for the new notes and instructions.

This tune will help you to practice the scale of C major.

Unto us a child is born

Piae Cantiones 1582

What key is this tune in?

Entry of the Clowns

Hawthorn

f

mf

mp

f

F

More in-between notes

Flat sign

On page 22 you found out about sharps. Another sort of in-between note is a flat. Flat notes are a semitone below their natural notes. You can see their symbol on the left.

Flat notes

The rungs are a semitone apart.

Each in-between note has a sharp and a flat name.

This note is F#.   This note is G♭.

Can you think of the two names for the note in between A and B?*

The note G flat is a semitone below G natural. You can see this on the small note ladder in the picture above.

G♭ can also be called F#. Even though they are the same note, they are written in different places on the staff.

The difference between sharps and flats

Here is a way to remember the difference between sharps and flats. "Mount Sharp" has a sharp point, and "Flat Plain" is flat.

Sharps are higher than flats.

Naturals are between sharps and flats.

Flats are lower than sharps.

Flat Plain

Mt. Sharp

Find out why in-between notes have two names on page 42.

Answer on page 63.

Playing and reading B♭ (or A#)

Play G on your recorder. Lift your left-hand middle finger and put down your right-hand first finger. This is B♭ or A#.

B♭

This note is A#.

The note B♭ is written on the middle line of the staff.

Play the bars below. Be especially careful when changing to and from B♭.

Getting louder and quieter

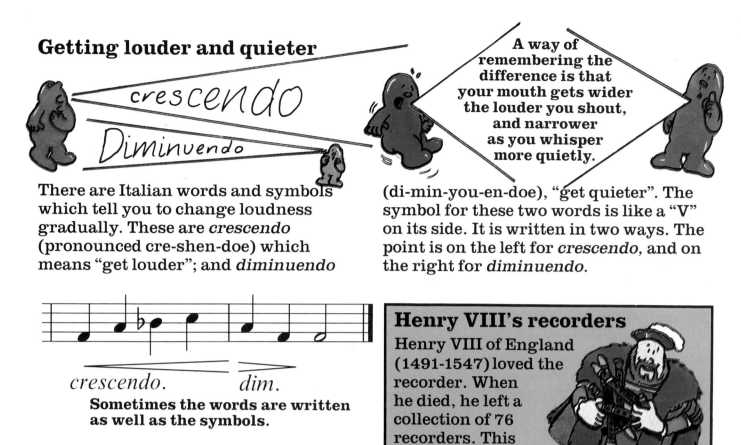

There are Italian words and symbols which tell you to change loudness gradually. These are *crescendo* (pronounced cre-shen-doe) which means "get louder"; and *diminuendo*

A way of remembering the difference is that your mouth gets wider the louder you shout, and narrower as you whisper more quietly.

(di-min-you-en-doe), "get quieter". The symbol for these two words is like a "V" on its side. It is written in two ways. The point is on the left for *crescendo*, and on the right for *diminuendo*.

crescendo.   *dim.*

Sometimes the words are written as well as the symbols.

You begin to get louder where the symbol starts, and stop when it ends. They can be long or short, depending on how quickly you have to change. For example, in the music above, you take a bar to get loud, but only two beats to get quiet again.

Henry VIII's recorders

Henry VIII of England (1491-1547) loved the recorder. When he died, he left a collection of 76 recorders. This included a box with silver fittings and crimson velvet containing eight recorders made of ivory.

Henry VIII wrote a lot of music for the recorder. There is some on page 59.

Tunes to play

Here is a tune to play. Look out for the key signature.

All through the night

Welsh

Bb

Tunes to play

The Holly and the Ivy

English

I saw three ships

English

My Bonnie lies over the ocean

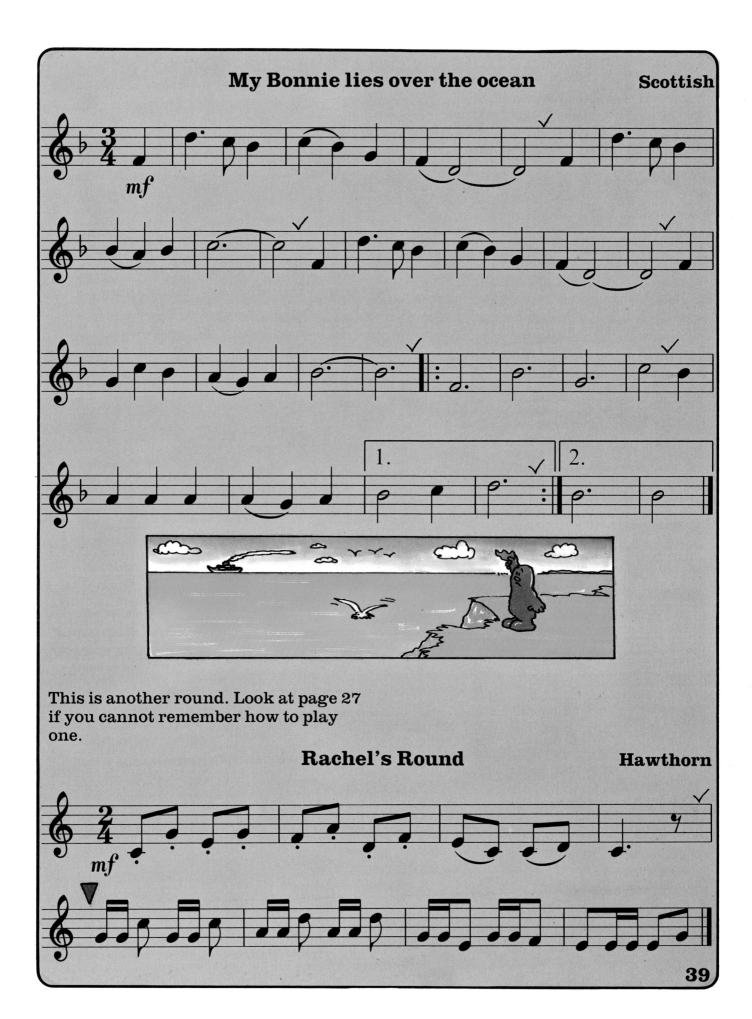

This is another round. Look at page 27
if you cannot remember how to play
one.

Rachel's Round

Hawthorn

More musical instructions

On these two pages you can learn more Italian words and symbols, and find out what they mean. There are also two new notes.

Playing quickly or slowly

The word for fast is *allegro*, pronounced "a-leg-roe". It is written above the staff. A folk dance may be played *allegro*.

The word for slowly is *lento* (len-toe). This is also written over the staff. A romantic tune may be played *lento*.

The speed between *allegro* and *lento* is *andante* (an-dan-tay). It means "at a walking pace".

The speed of a tune is known as its *tempo*. If a tune has a fast *tempo*, it is played quickly.

Getting slower

ritard   *a tempo*

Ritardando, pronounced "ri-ta-dan-doe", tells you to get slower. It is usually written under the staff as just *ritard*. The *tempo* slows down, just like a train slows down as it pulls into a station.

When *ritardando* occurs in the middle of a tune, it is often followed by *a tempo*. This tells you to return to the speed you were playing at before.

Pauses

When you see this sign over a note, you hold the note for a little longer than normal before you play the next one. You often see pauses at the end of a *ritardando* section.

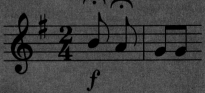

f

Pauses are often used in songs. There are two at the start of "The Grand Old Duke of York".

Italian repeat words

If you see *Da Capo* (often written *D.C.*) at the end of a tune, it means "play again from the beginning". You play everything again but ignore any repeat marks the second time.

Sometimes the words *al Fine* are written after *Da Capo*. This means that *Fine* (fee-nay) will be written on top of the staff somewhere in the tune. You play the tune again from the beginning, but stop when you get to *Fine*.

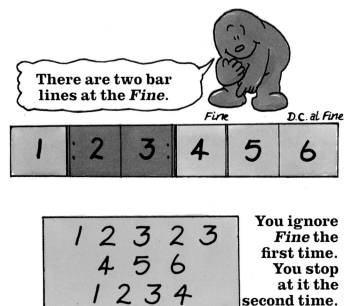

There are two bar lines at the *Fine*.

Fine   *D.C. al Fine*

| 1 | :2 | 3: | 4 | 5 | 6 |

1 2 3 2 3
4 5 6
1 2 3 4

You ignore *Fine* the first time. You stop at it the second time.

At the top are some numbered boxes. The green box shows the order in which you would play them.

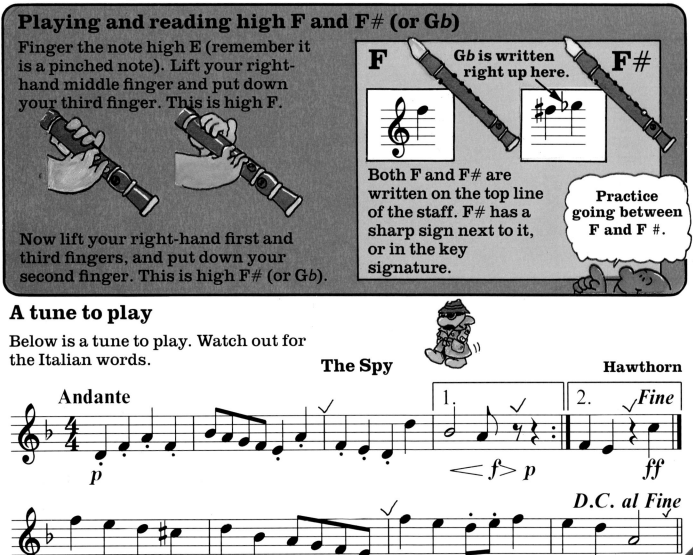

Playing and reading high F and F# (or G♭)

Finger the note high E (remember it is a pinched note). Lift your right-hand middle finger and put down your third finger. This is high F.

Now lift your right-hand first and third fingers, and put down your second finger. This is high F# (or G♭).

F   **F#**

G♭ is written right up here.

Both F and F# are written on the top line of the staff. F# has a sharp sign next to it, or in the key signature.

Practice going between F and F#.

A tune to play

Below is a tune to play. Watch out for the Italian words.

The Spy   Hawthorn

Andante

p   1. *<f> p*   2. *Fine*   *ff*

D.C. al Fine

F#
F#

More about scales

So far you have learned two scales: D major (on page 28) and C major (on page 35). On these two pages you can find how to work out which notes are in other major scales.

How to work out any scale

Every scale has eight notes, which are taken from the note ladder on page 24. The notes in each scale can be shown on their own smaller ladders.

There is one ladder for each scale. The ladders for C major and D major are shown in the picture below.

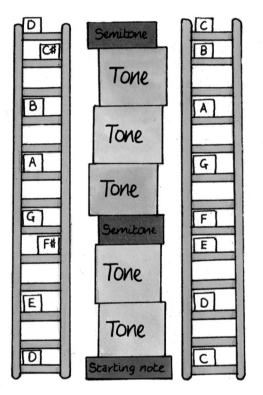

The intervals between each of the notes are shown by the piles of blocks next to the ladders. A red block shows a semitone and a yellow block, a tone.

As you can see, the pattern of tones and semitones are the same for both ladders.

The pattern is the same for any major scale. So the major scale for any note can be worked out by writing notes on a ladder in the correct order of intervals.

42

How to work out the scale of F major

Follow the steps below. You can work out any major scale like this.

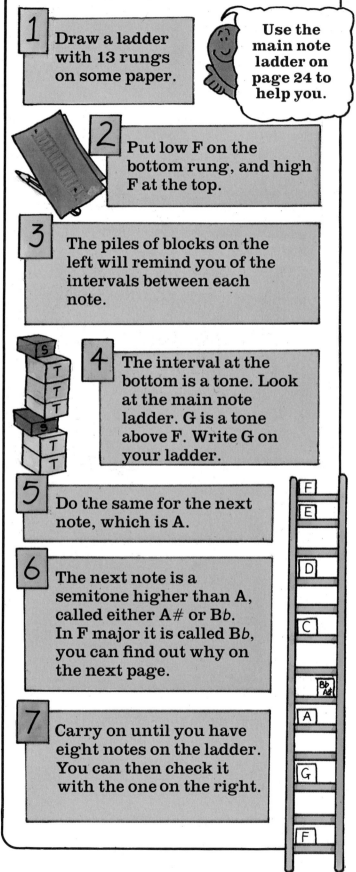

1 Draw a ladder with 13 rungs on some paper.

Use the main note ladder on page 24 to help you.

2 Put low F on the bottom rung, and high F at the top.

3 The piles of blocks on the left will remind you of the intervals between each note.

4 The interval at the bottom is a tone. Look at the main note ladder. G is a tone above F. Write G on your ladder.

5 Do the same for the next note, which is A.

6 The next note is a semitone higher than A, called either A# or B♭. In F major it is called B♭, you can find out why on the next page.

7 Carry on until you have eight notes on the ladder. You can then check it with the one on the right.

Naming in-between notes

Look at the scale ladders of D major and C major. They contain every letter-named note (some have in-between notes). This is true for every major scale. F major has an A, but no B note. So the fourth note is B♭. Every letter is now in the scale. You can see the scale on the right.

Tunes in the key of F major have a B♭ in the key signature.

This note is B♭ as there is no other "B" note in the scale.

F G A B♭ C D E F

A scale can have either sharps or flats. It never has both.

Practice playing the scale of F major.

Playing and reading high G

This is the highest note in this book. There are higher ones, but they are not played very often.

G'

High G is written in the space above the staff.

Finger the note high F# (see page 22). Now lift your right-hand middle finger. This is high G.

Practice the tune below to help you get used to the new note.

p <> *f*

p <> *ff*

The scale of G major

Try and work out the scale of G major following the same steps that you used for F major.

Hint: There is one in-between note in G major.

When you have worked out the notes, draw a staff and write them on it.

The scale of G major is shown on page 63. Look it up to check your answer.

G'

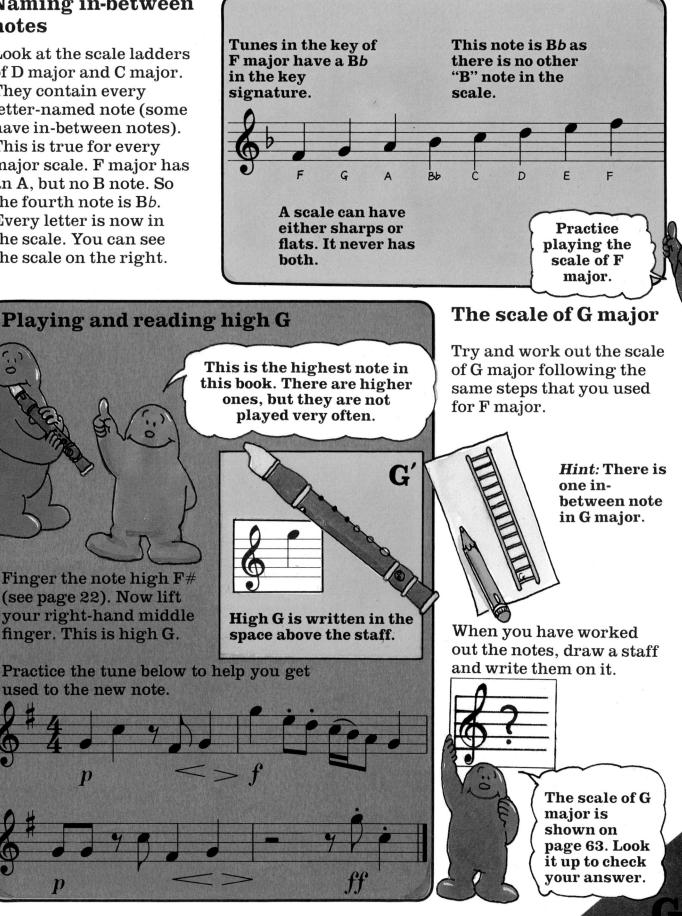

More notes to play

Below are four more notes. You will then be able to play every note on the main note ladder.

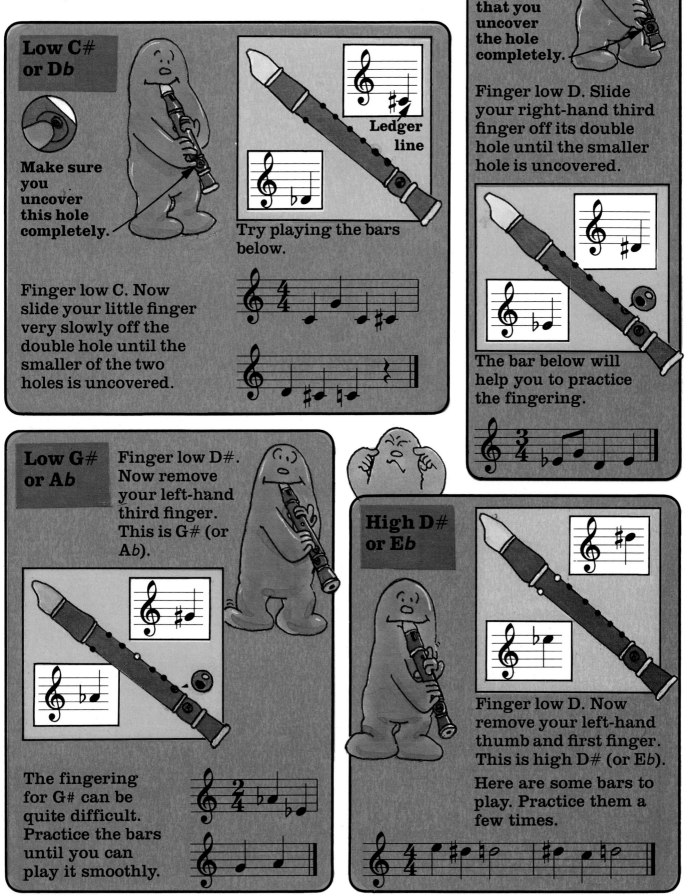

Low C# or Db

Make sure you uncover this hole completely.

Finger low C. Now slide your little finger very slowly off the double hole until the smaller of the two holes is uncovered.

Ledger line

Try playing the bars below.

Low D# or Eb

Make sure that you uncover the hole completely.

Finger low D. Slide your right-hand third finger off its double hole until the smaller hole is uncovered.

The bar below will help you to practice the fingering.

Low G# or Ab

Finger low D#. Now remove your left-hand third finger. This is G# (or Ab).

The fingering for G# can be quite difficult. Practice the bars until you can play it smoothly.

High D# or Eb

Finger low D. Now remove your left-hand thumb and first finger. This is high D# (or Eb).

Here are some bars to play. Practice them a few times.

A few tips on playing music

You have now learned enough about music to play all the tunes in this book. On this page are some tips to help you play them well.

Before you play

Don't start playing until you have made these checks.

1 Check the key signature

This will tell you which notes are sharps or flats.

2 Read through the music

This is so that you know which symbols and instructions are in the music. Below are a number of things to look out for.

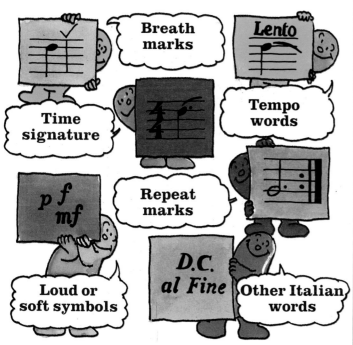

Time signature

Breath marks

Lento

Tempo words

p f mf

Repeat marks

D.C. al Fine

Loud or soft symbols

Other Italian words

Tap out the rhythm

Tapping the rhythm will help you to become familiar with the music, especially the harder parts.

Playing the tune

Once you have looked through the music, you are ready to start playing.

Play straight through

Play the tune without stopping, even if you make a mistake.

Practice

Practice the parts you found difficult. Play slowly at first, then build up speed.

Perform the tune

Once you can play the tune without any mistakes you are ready to play it to someone.

Make sure your fingering is accurate.

Remember how to stand (or sit) and hold your recorder (see page 6).

Lots more tunes

The next few pages have many different sorts of tunes for you to play and perform.

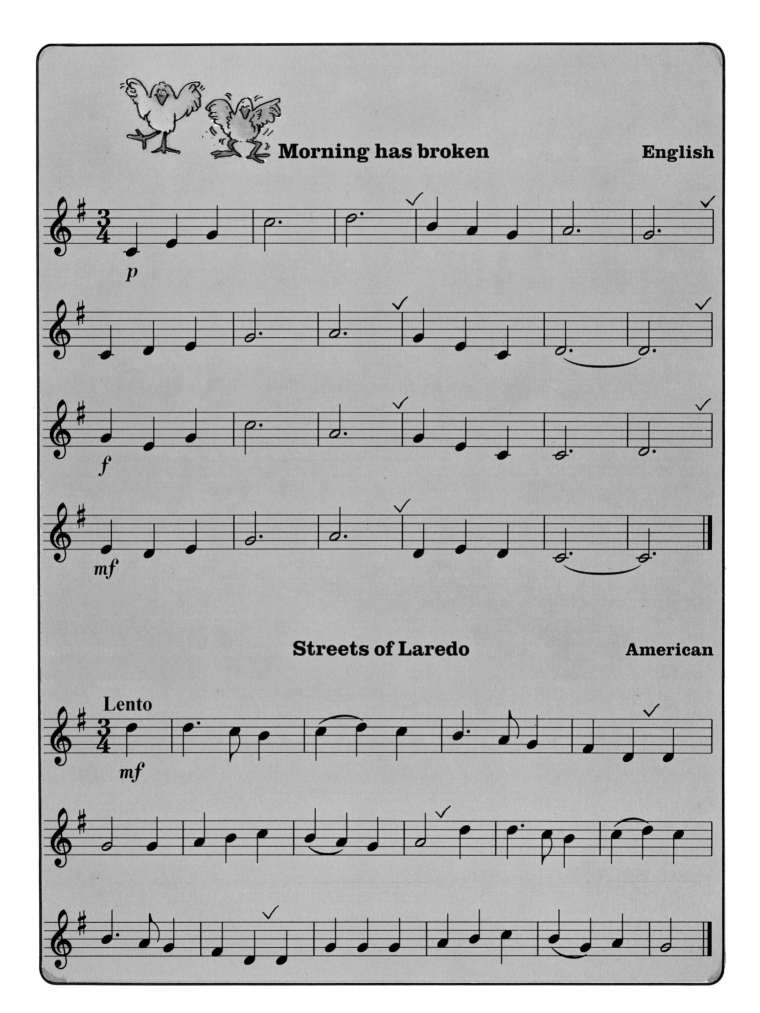

Morning has broken

English

Streets of Laredo

American

Familiar tunes

Tit Willow Sullivan

Scarborough Fair English

Arietta

Mozart

The Lincolnshire Poacher

Folk songs from Europe

Pat-a-pan

French

Auld Lang Syne

Scots

Rocking

Czech

Lord of all hopefulness

Irish

Tunes from classical music

There are four tunes taken from classical music pieces on these two pages.

The Blue Danube

Strauss

When Johnny comes marching home

Christmas carols

Good King Wenceslas   Piae Cantiones 1582

Hark! The herald angels sing   Mendelssohn

Il est né

French

We wish you a merry Christmas

English

Tunes for two players

These two tunes are called duets. (A tune for one player is called a solo). There is a staff of music for each player, unlike a round when there is only one. They are joined together, one on top of the other. Each one is called a part, labeled "1" or "2".

The parts are different, but they sound right when they are played together. Make sure that you and your music partner keep a steady beat.

Although these tunes are for two players, you can practice either part on your own.

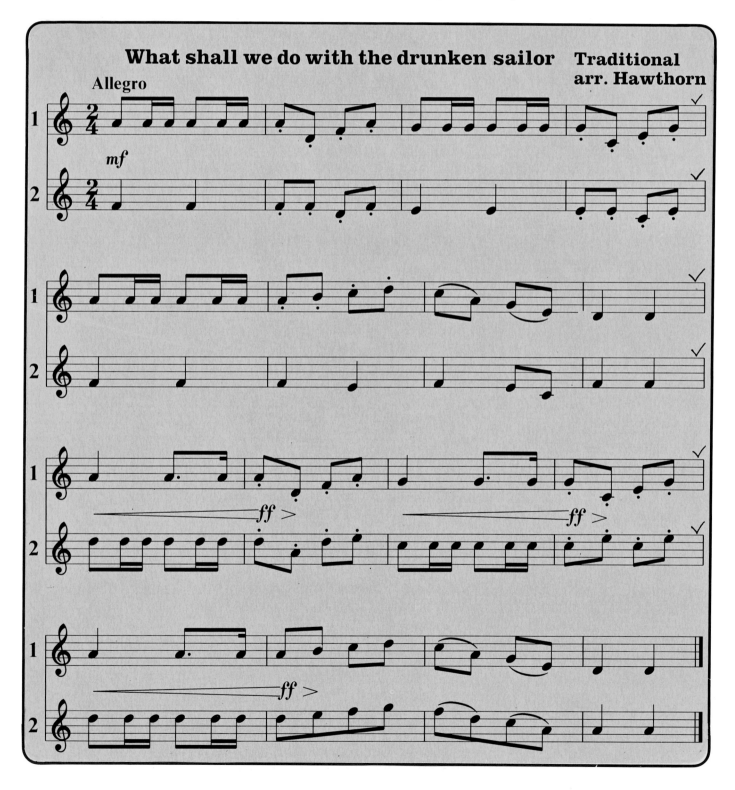

What shall we do with the drunken sailor
Traditional arr. Hawthorn

Mango Walk

Traditional

Tunes for recorder and piano

The top stave in the tunes below is for the recorder part. The bottom two are for the piano part. This is called the accompaniment. You can play the tune with or without the piano part.

Greensleeves

Pastime with Good Company

The recorder family

There are quite a few different sizes of recorder in the recorder family. The four most common ones are the sopranino, soprano, alto and tenor recorders. In the picture below, you can see their sizes relative to one another.

Tenor recorder

At 25 inches (64cm), this is the longest of the most common recorders. Its notes are an octave lower than the soprano's.

It has a support on the back for your right thumb as it is quite heavy. It has a key at the bottom to cover the lowest hole.

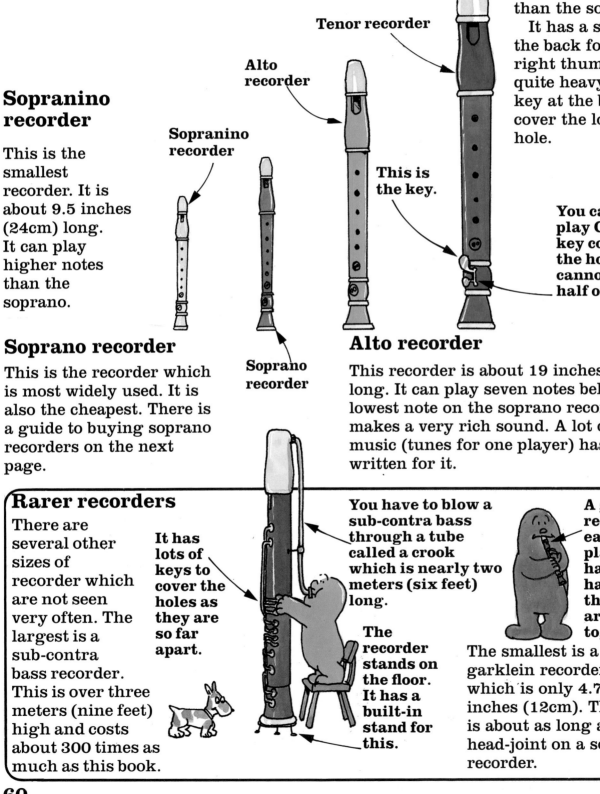

Tenor recorder

Alto recorder

Sopranino recorder

This is the key.

Soprano recorder

You cannot play C# as the key covers all the hole. You cannot cover half of it.

Sopranino recorder

This is the smallest recorder. It is about 9.5 inches (24cm) long. It can play higher notes than the soprano.

Soprano recorder

This is the recorder which is most widely used. It is also the cheapest. There is a guide to buying soprano recorders on the next page.

Alto recorder

This recorder is about 19 inches (48cm) long. It can play seven notes below the lowest note on the soprano recorder. It makes a very rich sound. A lot of solo music (tunes for one player) has been written for it.

Rarer recorders

There are several other sizes of recorder which are not seen very often. The largest is a sub-contra bass recorder. This is over three meters (nine feet) high and costs about 300 times as much as this book.

It has lots of keys to cover the holes as they are so far apart.

You have to blow a sub-contra bass through a tube called a crook which is nearly two meters (six feet) long.

The recorder stands on the floor. It has a built-in stand for this.

A garklein recorder is easier to play if you have small hands as the holes are so close together.

The smallest is a garklein recorder, which is only 4.75 inches (12cm). This is about as long as the head-joint on a soprano recorder.

Buying a soprano recorder

A soprano recorder is one of the cheapest musical instruments you can buy. Below is a table of some well-known brands. It tells you whether they are made of plastic or wood and how many joints they have.

The prices vary from just under the cost of this book to over 30 times as much. The recorders get more expensive as you go down the table. The cheapest is at the top, the most expensive at the bottom.

Recorders on record

Below are some records of recorder music which you can buy. The record labels and numbers are in brackets.

Recorder Recital
by Michaela Petri
(BBC Records REC 298)

Telemann Sonatas
by Michaela Petri
(Philips 9500 941)

Sonatas by Handel and Telemann
by Franz Brüggen
(Telefunken DX 635359)

Handel Sonata Opus 1
by Hans-Martin Linde
(EMI IC0659 9720)

Works by Vivaldi, Marcello (and others)
by Philip Picket
(Saga 5465)

Make of recorder	Wooden or plastic	Number of joints
Yamaha	plastic	3
Milton	plastic	2
Boosey & Hawkes	wooden	2
Aulos*	plastic	3
Zen-on*	plastic	3
Dolmetsch	plastic	3
Adler*	wooden	2
Hohner*	plastic	1 or 2
Schott	wooden	2
Musima	wooden	2
Hohner*	wooden	2
Hellinger	wooden	2
Moeck*	wooden	2
Mollenhauer*	wooden	2
Kung*	wooden	2
Moeck* (hand-made)	wooden	2
Dolmetsch* (hand-made)	wooden	2

These two companies also make a range of recorders like those of the 16th century, called renaissance recorders.

Renaissance tenor recorder

It is best to buy recorders from a music store. You may find cheaper ones in other stores, but often they do not sound very good and can be harder to play.

*This means that there is a range of models at different prices. The place in the table is for the cheapest model.

Recorder and music words

Below is a list of explanations for some of the music words which have been used in this book. The list is in alphabetical order. When an explanation includes another music word, the word is shown in dark type. This means that it is explained elsewhere on the page.

A tempo Play the music at the original **tempo** (speed).

Allegro Play the music fast.

Anacrusis Part of a bar at the beginning of a piece of music.

Andante Play the music at a walking pace.

Bar Section of music between two upright lines on the **staff**. It contains the number of **beats** indicated in the **time signature**.

Beat This word has many different meanings. In this book it describes a note of **quarter note** length.

Breath mark Symbol which shows you where to breathe in the music.

Crescendo Get louder as you play the next part of the music.

Da Capo al Fine Go back to the beginning of the music and play it again until you get to the word **Fine**.

Diminuendo Get quicker as you play the next part of the music.

Dotted note **Note** followed by a dot. The dot makes it half as long again.

Duet Piece of music for two players. There is a separate **staff** for each player.

Eighth note **Note** which last for half a **beat**.

Fine End of the music. See **Da Capo al Fine**.

Fingering Covering holes in order to play certain **notes**.

Flat note **Note** which is a **semitone** below the **natural** of the same name.

Half note A **note** two **beats** long.

In-between note A **sharp** or **flat note**.

Interval Distance between two **notes** (see **Tone** and **Semitone**).

Key Letter name of a **scale** indicated by a **key signature**.

Key signature **Sharps** or **flats** written at the beginning of the music.

Ledger line Extra lines for **notes** that are too high or low for the **staff**.

Lento Play the music slowly.

Natural note **Note** which is named after a letter between A and G (its letter-name). It is not a **sharp** or **flat note**.

Note A musical sound. Notes vary according to how high or low they are (shown by their positions on the **staff**), and how long they are (shown by the note symbol).

Octave **Interval** between a **note** and the next one with the same letter name.

Pause sign Tells you to leave a short gap in the music.

Pinching Uncovering a small part of the thumb hole by bending the thumb.

Quarter note A **note** one **beat** long.

Repeat mark Symbol which tells you to play either a section or all of the **tune** again.

Rest Symbol which replaces a **note** in a **bar**. Tells you to leave a gap lasting for a number of **beats**.

Rhythm **Note** lengths which make up the music.

Ritardando Get gradually slower as you play the next part of the music.

Round Tune for two players written on one **staff**. Each player starts playing at a different time.

Scale Series of eight **notes** which have a set pattern of **intervals** between them. The first and last **notes** are an octave apart.

Semitone The smallest **interval** between two **notes**, for example G and G#.

Sharp note Note which is a **semitone** above the **natural note** of the same name.

Sixteenth note Half an **eighth note**.

Slur Line which links two or more **notes** at different places on the **staff**. You **tongue** the first note only.

Staff Set of five lines on which music is written.

Tempo Speed of a **tune**.

Tie Line which links two or more **notes** on the same line or space. You add the lengths of the **notes** together.

Time signature Numbers at the start of a piece of music which tell you how many **beats** are in each **bar**. Also tells you how long the **beats** are.

Tone Interval of two **semitones**, for example betweeen G and A.

Tonguing Starting a **note** using your tongue to say "too".

Treble clef Symbol at the beginning of each **staff** of **soprano** recorder music.

Tune Series of **notes** written on a **staff**.

Whole note Note which is four **beats** long.

Answers

p. 11 There are four bars in the tune.

If the last bar contained only quarter notes, there would be four of them.

p. 16 A rhythm which you tap does not have to be on a staff as the beats do not have letter-names.

p. 17 The last bar would contain two beats if the anacrusis was two beats.

p. 18 The tied note on the left has seven beats. The one on the right has five beats.

p. 21 The orders in which you would play the bars are:

1 2 3 4   5 6 5 6

1 2 1 2   3 4 5 5

1 2 3 1 2 3   4 5 4 5

p. 24 There are 20 different notes on the note ladder.

Notes E and F and notes B and C do not have sharp notes between them.

p. 31 You tongue all legato notes, but you only tongue the first note in a group of slurred notes.

p. 35 The tune is in the key of C major.

p. 36 The two names for the note in between A and B are A# and B♭.

p. 43 Below are the notes in the scale of G major. There is an F# in the key signature.

Index

Notes							
B	— 8	C′	— 21	C	— 33	G′	— 42
A	— 12	F#	— 22	F	— 34	C#	— 44
G	— 14	C#′	— 24	B♭	— 36	D#	— 44
E	— 16	D′	— 25	F′	— 41	D#′	— 44
D	— 18	E′	— 29	F#′	— 41	G#	— 44

Usborne Publishing Ltd would like to thank the following for allowing their copyright material to be used in this book:

Westminster Music Ltd – for Streets of London by Ralph McTell © 1968.